Little Duck

Stories with children's wellbeing at heart
www.traceythomson.com

Little Duck on the river
swimming round and around

Looks into the water
and what has he found?

A Fish swims beneath him
down deep all day long

"I wish I could swim there
I wish I was strong"

Little Duck on the river
swimming round and around

Looks up at the clouds
and what has he found?

A Bird flies above him
so high in the sky

"I wish I could fly there
I really must try"

Little Duck on the river
swimming round and around
Looks into the trees
and what has he found?

A squirrel is climbing
so brave and so true

"I wish I could climb there
I wish I was you"

Little Duck on the river
swimming round and around
Looks out at the riverbank
and what has he found?

A frog jumps all over
on rocks by a tree

"I wish I could jump there
I wish that was me"

Little Duck on the river
wishing that he could be

someone else for a while
someone strong and carefree

He must paddle like crazy
round in circles each day

While the others all seem
to have spare time to play

The Fish in the water
swimming round and around

Looks up from beneath
and what has he found?

A Duck glides above him
so carefree and strong

"I wish I could swim there
have fun all day long"

The Bird in the clouds
flying round and around

Looks down at the river
and what has he found?

A Duck drifts below him
there's no need to fly

"I wish I could rest there
I really must try"

The Squirrel in the tree
climbing round and around

Looks onto the river
and what has he found?

A Duck on the water
so graceful and true

"I wish I could float there
I wish I was you"

The Frog on the rocks
jumping round and around
Looks out from the riverbank
and what has he found?

A Duck paddles over
so happy and free
"I wish I could play there
I wish that was me"

Little Duck on the river
stops swimming around

He is still for a moment
and what has he found?

He stops
watching
others
and then
he can see

"I'm happy
with my life

it's good
to be me"

Stay strong
Little Duck

Be brave
and be true

The best thing
about you

Is that you are
YOU

For my family

with love x

Tracey x

other books by the author

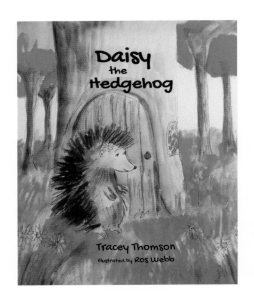

Stories with children's wellbeing at heart

www.traceythomson.com

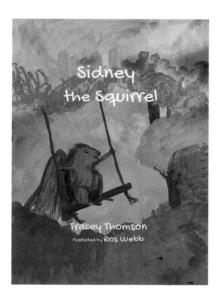

**Sidney
the Squirrel**

Tracey Thomson

Illustrated by Ros Webb

Sidney the Squirrel

is hyperactive and struggles to concentrate
but he needs to focus to gather food
as winter approaches.

How will he prepare for the cold
months ahead with so many
distractions?

Maybe there's a surprise
in store for his friends...

stories with children's wellbeing at heart

www.traceythomson.com

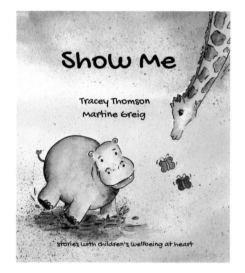

Show Me

Tracey Thomson
Martine Greig

stories with children's wellbeing at heart

Show Me...

a collection of animal rhyming verses
which encourage young children
to move around and have fun

Can you run as fast as a cheetah? Or jump as
high as a frog? Maybe you can waddle like
a penguin or stand on one leg like a flamingo?

Grown ups can join in too!

stories with children's wellbeing at heart
www.traceythomson.com

Printed in Great Britain
by Amazon